KURT WIESE

HAPPY EASTER

PUFFIN BOOKS

PUFFIN BOOKS
A Division of Penguin Books USA, Inc.
375 Hudson Street, New York, New York 10014
Penguin Books Ltd, 27 Wrights Lane, London W8 5TZ, England
Penguin Books Australia Ltd, Ringwood, Victoria, Australia
Penguin Books Canada Ltd, 10 Alcorn Avenue, Toronto, Ontario, Canada M4V 3B2
Penguin Books (N.Z.) Ltd, 182-190 Wairau Road, Auckland 10, New Zealand

Penguin Books Ltd, Registered Offices: Harmondsworth, Middlesex, England

First published in the United States of America by Viking Penguin Inc., 1952
Published in Picture Puffins, 1989
5   7   9   10   8   6
Copyright Kurt Wiese, 1952
Copyright © renewed Gertrude Wiese, 1980
All rights reserved

LIBRARY OF CONGRESS CATALOGING IN PUBLICATION DATA
Wiese, Kurt. 1887-
Happy Easter / by Kurt Wiese.   p.   cm.—(Picture Puffins)
Summary: Mama Rabbit sends her children out to fetch eggs for
Easter, but when the rabbits begin to paint them, they are greeted by a colorful surprise.
ISBN 0-14-050977-1
[1. Rabbits—Fiction.]   1. Title.
PZ7.W636Hap   1989   [E]—dc19   88-28804   CIP

Printed in the United States of America
Set in Lydian

"Go and get me some eggs," said the mother rabbit to her two children.

"Hurry," she said. "There is only one day left to color the eggs and hide them in people's gardens."

So the children started off.

They hurried as they were told

down the hill to where the hen lived.

"Good morning," said the rabbits to the hen, who sat on her nest with her feathers all spread.

"Good morning. Could we have some eggs?

"We are in a hurry because there is only one day left to color the eggs and hide them in people's gardens."

First the hen said, "No!"—but

the rabbits pleaded and pleaded, till at last the hen said,

"All right, you can have these. I have been sitting on them for three whole weeks and not one will hatch."

So she helped the rabbit children

to put the eggs in their baskets,

and then they went home.

Meanwhile at home the mother rabbit had prepared everything to color the eggs and soon

the whole family was painting eggs with the colors which had been
left by the last rainbow.

They sat and painted and sat and painted and looked at their
work and then it happened—

Listen! There was a crickle here and a crackle there—

and the noise came from the eggs!

"Pop!" it went—and the egg in the mother rabbit's paw burst open and out came a chicken!

"Pop—pop—pop!" popped from everywhere and all the eggs cracked open and out of every one came a chicken colored like the egg it came from.

Just then the hen came up to the door of the rabbits' house to see how the eggs would look in color, and there she saw all the little chickens.

So she said, "Glook, glook," and the chickens all came running
to her,

and she led them home.

The rabbits looked after them—

and there were no Easter eggs that year,

BUT—

oh, such beautiful chickens!